Richard Scarry's
Busiest People Ever

Richard Scarry's
Busiest People Ever

First published in 1976
This edition published by HarperCollins *Children's Books* in 2013
HarperCollins Children's Books is a division of HarperCollins Publishers Ltd,
77-85 Fulham Palace Road, London W6 8JB

1 3 5 7 9 10 8 6 4 2

ISBN:978-0-00-793669-4

The HarperCollins website address is www.harpercollins.co.uk

Printed and bound in China.

HarperCollins *Children's Books*

The busy people are on their way to work.
Bre-e-e-et! Sergeant Murphy blows his whistle to
stop the traffic and let the workers cross the street.

Bre-e-e-e-t! Lowly Worm and Huckle Cat are helping Sergeant Murphy direct traffic. Lowly and Huckle want to be policemen when they grow up.

Miney and Moe, the television camera bugs, take pictures of things that happen in Busytown. The pictures will be part of a television programme.

vicar

TELEVISIONS

BOOKS

bookseller

optician

SPORTS

SPECTACLES

SPORT SHOP

Sergeant Murphy rides around town to make sure everything is peaceful.

If the Chief of Police hears of any trouble, he tells Sergeant Murphy about it over the radio.

"Sergeant Murphy! Sergeant Murphy!" The police station is calling Murphy on the radio. "Grocer Cat has just telephoned. His grocery store has been robbed!" "Quickly! We must try to catch the thief!" says Sergeant Murphy.

road painter

ditch digger

SHOEMAKER

Get off that fresh cement, Mr. Frumble!

FRESH CEMENT

radio operator

POLICE STATION

DELICATESSEN

CONFECTIONERY

Chief of Police

CHEMIST

HARDWARE

HATS

FLOWERS

chemist

ICE CREAM

ice-cream seller

EAT HATS

sandwich-board person

flower seller

ELECTRIC SUPPLIES

GROCERIES

BANANAS

APPLES

ORANGES

TV

Grocer Cat

Sergeant Murphy speeds
through the street on his
motorcycle.
"Faster, faster!" says Lowly.
"We must catch the thief."

postman

fireman

road sweeper

Stop thief!

miner

rug salesman

locksmith

violinist

TV repairman

bugdozer driv

drummer

building worker

American
football play

golfer

brush salesman

magician

floris

"Look!" says Sergeant Murphy. "The thief must be
in that crowd of people. All of them are carrying things.
How can we tell which one stole something
from Grocer Cat's store?"
Lowly looks at the crowd and suddenly shouts,
"There's the thief!"

Lowly chases after the
thief and tackles him
around the legs.
Who can it be?

billboard paster

juggler

architect

lifeguard

street cleaner

lawyer

banana eater

plumber

soldier

ailor

double bass player

carpenter

tennis player

window cleaner

another tennis player

It's Bananas Gorilla! And Lowly has caught him.
"But how did you know Bananas was the thief?"
asks Sergeant Murphy.
"Well," says Lowly, "out of all those people Bananas
was the only one carrying something that
could be stolen from a grocery store."
Very good thinking, Policeman Lowly.
Take Bananas off to jail now.

A Visit to the Big City

Mother Cat is taking Huckle and Lowly to the city. What do you think they are going to do there? They have to take the train. Mother Cat sits in the passenger coach. Huckle and Lowly sit with the driver of the engine. *To-o-o-o-t!* Lowly pulls the whistle. Off they go.

bulb changer

taxi driver

travelling salesman

skier

scout leader

porter

mountain climber

scouts

signalman

cook

waiter

passengers

DINING CAR

COAC

wheel tapper

BUSYTOWN

NEWSPAPERS

BAGGA

TICKETS

TIME TABLE

ticket seller

newsagent

baggage checker

fork-lift truck operator

station master

snack-cart attendant

sandwich eater

conductor

oiler

truck driver

bricklayer

mechanical
shovel

bulldozer operator

plumber   carpenters

plumber

bricklayer

HOUSES
FOR
SALE

mortar mixer

bathtub
deliverymen

driver

newspaper
reader

carpenters

roofer

electrician

painter

paper-hanger

nail spiller

gardener

cooker and
refrigerator
deliveryman

SOLD

TV

The train chugs along the tracks on
the way to the big city.
Suddenly Lowly shouts,
"STOP! Something is wrong!"
The train stops. Lowly jumps down from the
locomotive and runs to the switch.
What can the matter be?

driver

school bus
driver

log cutter

log hauler

tree chopper

kite flier

grass mower

A goods train is speeding towards them on the same line.
Lowly moves the switch… just in time!
The goods train rolls onto another line. Lowly has
saved everyone from a terrible accident.
Lowly is certainly a good railway worker, isn't he?

Watch out,
Mr. Frumble!

ICE
CREAM

TRAVEL

FLY

COME TO PLAND

GIFT SHOP

LEFT LUGGAGE

FLOWER

MAIL

luggage trolley driver

PLAT 3

PLATFORM 2

sleeping car

workers running to catch their train

sweeper

PLATFORM 1

SNACK BAR

NEWSAGENT

window
cleaner

clock fixer

TV

EXIT

jewellery seller

TICKETS

TIMETABLE

TO TAXIS

porter

pencil seller

Finally the train arrives at the
city's railway station.
What a big, busy place it is!
Look! Someone is there to greet
the three arrivals. Who can he be?

steel
workers

nosy pedestrian

welder

crane operator

site
manager

cement
mixer

NOW BUILDING
A NEW
SKYSCRAPER

TV1

A television producer has come to meet
them. A few days ago he had invited
Huckle and Lowly to appear on his
television show. He drives them through
the city streets to the television studio.

musicians

camera operator

In the television studio, Huckle and Lowly sing a jolly song. People all over the country can see and hear the programme on their television sets.

When Huck and Lowly return to Busytown, all their friends will tell them that they saw the programme, too.

Grandma Cat lives far away, but she sees Huckle and Lowly on her television set. She is very surprised and pleased. "I must visit my two television entertainers soon," she says. Would YOU like to be a television singer, too?

Mr. Frumble's Bad Day

Mr. Frumble is going to work.
He forgot to open the garage
doors before he reversed the car.
What a bad way to start the day!

butcher

cashier

manager

There are a few things Mr.
Frumble must do on his way
to work. First, he stops to
shop at the supermarket.
Look at what he's done now!

book borrowers

librarian

Next, he goes to the library to borrow a book.
The librarian does not like noisy sneezers.

barber

At the barbershop he fidgets so much
that the barber cuts his tie by mistake.

chemist

Mr. Frumble has a little accident when he
buys some vitamins from the chemist.

Then he tries on a suit at the clothing store.
"I think you need a larger size, Mr. Frumble."

He tries on a hat. "Don't pull it
down so hard, Mr. Frumble."

launderette attendant

He washes his laundry at the launderette.
"I think you have put too much soap in the machine, Mr. Frumble."

nurse

At Dr. Lion's office he breaks the scales. Does Mr. Frumble weigh THAT much?

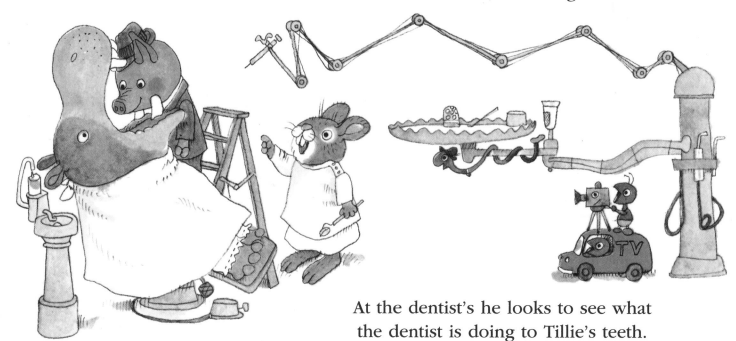

At the dentist's he looks to see what
the dentist is doing to Tillie's teeth.
"Please sit down and wait your turn, Mr. Frumble."

waitress

chef

waiter

Mr. Frumble goes into a restaurant to eat his lunch.
He sees the chef cooking some Flambéed Bananas.

Mr. Frumble thinks the fire is
dangerous. He throws water on it.

The chef is furious.
"I NEED fire to cook my bananas," he
says. "Now you have ruined them."

The angry chef frightens Mr. Frumble.
He runs out of the restaurant.
Oops! Watch where you are going, Mr.Frumble.

teacher

pupils

post-office clerk

DRIVE-IN BANK

SCHOOL

POST OFFICE

Bananamobile driver

bank cashier

Mr. Frumble gets back into his car, but again he doesn't look where he is going. He runs into a water hydrant and accidentally puts out another fire on the chef's Flambéed Bananas.

photographer

paperboy

reporter

typist

edito

THE DAILY EAGLE

MUSIC SHOP

RESTAURANT

OUR SPECIALITY—
FLAMBÉED BANANAS

chimney
sweep

AUTOMOBILES

BICYCLES

THE
COFFEE
POT

car salesman

newspaper
deliveryman

NEWSPAPER
DELIVERY

typesetter

printers

bulldozer operator

bugdozer operator

road layer

dump-truck driver

PETROL

Mr. Frumble! How did you ever get
your car on that new road?
It's not ready yet for drivers.
The workers are still busy building it.
Get off immediately. You have certainly had a
bad day, haven't you, Mr. Frumble?

pumpkin car driver

petrol pump attendant

car greaser

road-roller operator

dump-truck driver

"It's about time you went home," Lowly tells Mr. Frumble, "before you cause any more trouble. I will call a breakdown truck for you."

breakdown truck driver

pilot

A breakdown truck comes and takes Mr. Frumble home. So long, Mr. Frumble. You didn't even get to work today. Maybe things will be better tomorrow.

lightship
captain

tugboat skipper

crane
operator

helmsman

ship
capt

lobster
fisherman

straddle-carrier
driver

fork-lift
truck
driver

taxi driver

TAXI

TAXI

Down by the Busy Sea

radio operator

coastguard

waiter

purser

passengers

ship's painter

Huckle and Lowly are visiting Captain Salty down at the pier.
The captain shows them all the things there are to see at a harbour.
"This is a passenger ship," he explains. "It will carry people across the
ocean to visit their friends in distant places."
Lowly thinks he would like to be a sea captain when he grows up.

lighthouse
keeper

sailor

fishermen

Next, Captain Salty points to a cargo ship.
"It can carry all kinds of things to distant ports," he says.
"Just now cars are being loaded into its hold.
The ship will carry them across the sea and people
in faraway countries will drive them."
"LOOK!" cries Captain Salty loudly.
"There is a fire on that barge. We must
help! Hop onto the fireboat. Let's go!"

captain

fireboat

stevedores

fork-lift truck
driver

harbour police

giant-crane operator

dockside train driver

submarine skipper

Mr. Frumble, the boat wrecker

The fireboat rushes towards the burning barge and sprays it with water.

fireboat

ferry-boat captain

FERRY

fireboat

lazy fisherman

Captain Tillie has jumped off the burning barge.
"Help! Help!" she cries.
Lowly jumps overboard with
a life belt to save her.

A wet Captain Tillie thanks Lowly and gives
him a big kiss. Isn't it amazing that such a little
fellow can rescue such a big sea captain?
Good work, Sea Captain Lowly.

hay baler

tractor driver

cabbage picker

farm hand

grass mower

poster paster

woodcutter

fence builder

wall builder

hay lifter

Grandma Cat Comes to Visit

Grandma Cat is coming to visit the Cat family.
The whole family drives to the airport to meet her.
As the car passes Farmer Goat's farm, Lowly asks,
"Can we stop and buy some apples?"
Father Cat says, "No. We don't want to be late arriving at the airport."

surveyor

windmill fixer

lightning rod installer

apple picker

apple gatherer

corn picker

APPLES

apple seller

apple sauce cooker

water pumper

pumpkin seller

glider pilot

They arrive at the airport
ahead of time. While they wait for
Grandma's plane to come in, Lowly visits
the flight compartment of a plane that will
soon take off. Now he would like to be an
aeroplane pilot instead of a sea captain.
Huckle visits the airport control tower. He
would like to be an air-traffic controller and
tell the planes when to land and take off.

helicopter pilot

air-traffic controller

radar controller

ground controller

weatherman

What would YOU like to do at an airport.

pilot

LOUNGE

co-pilot

flight engineer

flight attendant

pilot

BUSYTOWN AIRPORT

TO ALL FLIGHTS

CHECK-IN COUNTER

TAXI

Mr. Frumble, the upside-down pilot

parachutist

balloonist

FOLLOW ME

aeroplane washer

stewardess

SWISSAIR

postman

luggage porter

FUEL

AIR MAIL POST OFFICE

Here comes Grandma's plane now.
But why is she travelling on a big cargo plane?
Why isn't she on a passenger plane?

Mr. Frumble! You're washing the wrong plane!

food-delivery person

Well! It seems that Grandma was bringing so many apples with her that she had to come on a cargo plane. Grandma plans to make lots of apple pies on her visit.
"Hi, Grandma. It's good to see you," says Huckle.
"And all your apples, too," says Lowly.

Busy House Workers

Grandma is happy to be visiting so many busy workers.

Lowly works hard to make his bed.

Huckle works to tidy his room.

Little Sister empties a wastebasket.

Daddy washes the dirty dishes.

Mummy cooks the meals for the family.

And Grandma and Lowly work hard making lots of apple pies to eat. Lowly is especially good at peeling apples.

While the apple pies are baking in the oven, they all watch the television news of the week.

They see Lowly, the policeman, capturing Bananas Gorilla.

They see Lowly, the railway worker, saving the train.

They see Huckle and Lowly singing on television.

They see Lowly, the sea captain, saving Captain Tillie.

After seeing all those jobs, Lowly, what would you like best of all to be when you grow up?
"Why," says Lowly, "I think best of all I would like to be an apple-pie eater."
Well, Lowly, I think that is very nice work indeed.

Would YOU like to help Lowly eat apple pies?